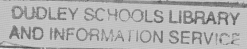

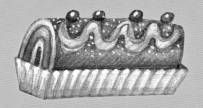

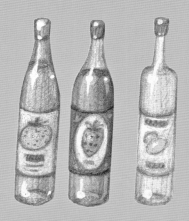

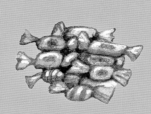

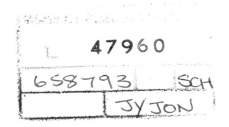
To Aileen - M.J.
To Michela - M.E.

First published in the United Kingdom in 2005
by Ragged Bears Publishing Limited, Milborne Wick,
Sherborne, Dorset DT9 4PW
www.raggedbears.co.uk

Distributed by Ragged Bears Limited, Nightingale House,
Queen Camel, Somerset
BA22 7NN. Tel: 01935 851590

Text copyright © 2005 Merlin Jones
Illustrations copyright © 2005 Mauro Evangelista
The rights of Merlin Jones and Mauro Evangelista to be
identified as author and illustrator of this work have been asserted

A CIP record of this book is available from the British Library

ISBN hardback 1 85714 289 6
ISBN paperback 1 85714 290 X

Printed in China

When The Lions Came to Tea

By Merlin Jones
Illustrated by Mauro Evangelista

RAGGED BEARS
Milborne Wick, Dorset

Said Jumpin' Jack, the Kangaroo

'Next week our Joey's three -

We'll have a birthday party,

And ask his friends to tea.'

Little Joey clapped his paws,

And jumped around in joy -

He dearly loved a party,

And was a jumping sort of boy!

So down to Mr Chimp's big store
Joey's mum went hopping,
To find some invitation cards
And do the party shopping.

She had so many things to buy,

Her pouch was full of money

For cakes and sweets and lemonade

And chocolates and honey

And paper hats and big balloons

- the party would be fun -

And neatly wrapped in cellophane

A prize for everyone.

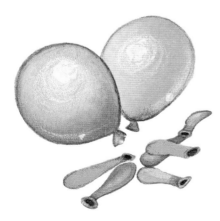

Jack sat down to write a list.

'There's **Mr. Chimp's** small boy,

the **Hippo** girls, the **Leopard** lads,

And of course your cousin Roy.

And **Elephant Al** - your biggest pal!

And **Kenneth Cockatoo**,

And **Tiny Tim** the Capuchin,

With his little sister Sue.

George Giraffe, Bertie Bear,

Miss Twinkletoes the deer.

- But we'll have to leave the **Lions** out,

We dare not have them here.

They'd frighten all the other guests,
There'd be a dreadful fuss -
Instead of eating cakes and things
They'd start by eating us!'

'Oh goodness me,' said Mrs Jack,
'What a difficult situation,
The Lions will be furious if
They get no invitation.'

But Jumpin' Jack was very firm -
'They're much too dangerous,
And as I said before, my dear,
I don't want them eating us!'

So Joey's mum then took the cards

To the postman, Mr Crow.

And asked him to be kind enough

To go and fly quite low,

Over the homes of all those friends,

And drop each one a card,

And to be quite certain that

It fell into their yard.

Now Mr Crow was a nice old bird,

But he wasn't very bright,

And he really didn't notice when

He dropped one card in flight,

For it slipped from his bag and floated down

Curving through the air,

Till finally it came to rest

Right next to the Lions' lair !

The King of Beasts lay in the shade,

A pleasant place to lie on,

At play nearby were his two cubs,

Len and Leo Lion.

They pulled their father's tail and yelled

'Look Dad, what we've found -

An invitation to a party,

Lying here upon the ground!'

Their father said, 'I'm quite surprised

That we were asked at all,

So look forward to this lucky chance

-We're going to have a ball!'

When party-time at last came round,

They were feeling most excited,

And groomed their manes to look their best,

Though they hadn't been invited!

Meanwhile, back at Jumpin' Jack's,

Everyone was there,

Eating the food, or running around,

Chasing Bertie Bear.

Elephant Al was giving a ride

To the two Capuchin twins,

And little Joe was larking about,

Throwing banana skins.

Jumpin' Jack was looking on,

With a wide smile on his face,

Everyone was having fun,

That day at the Kangaroos' place.

When suddenly there was a hush,

And **DANGER** was in the air,

And everyone stopped, and turned and stared -

The Lions **were standing there!!**

Though stiff with fright, Jack forced a smile,

And spoke up bright and hearty,

'Ah, welcome to you all, my friends,

Welcome to our party!'

The Lion replied, with a gracious bow,

'Sir, we are delighted,

It's all too rare, I can't think why,

For us to be invited.'

Len and Leo also bowed,

And quickly said their thanks,

They were eager to go and join the show

And all the fun and pranks.

Jack said, 'You must have travelled far,

Across the wide savannah,

Please do have lots and lots to eat,

- Pray try this ripe banana!'

(He was glad to see they liked the cakes,

The buns and all the rest,

And did not seem at all inclined

To eat a single guest!)

With paper hats upon their heads

The Lions were ready to play

And Joey's friends were not afraid

Of Leo and Len that day.

Miss Twinkletoes the Antelope

Chased them round a tree,

It really was the strangest sight

That ever you did see.

The Hippo girls performed a dance,

Twirling round and round,

When their great hooves came crashing down

They really shook the ground!

Little Sue and Tiny Tim,

Their arms around each other

Came very shyly up to Len,

And kissed him and his brother!

The jollity went on all day

And Jack was glad to see

That Leo and Len, like gentlemen,

Behaved most properly.

Mr Jack said to Mrs Jack

'There you are, my dear,

As I told you all along

We had nothing at all to fear.

However bad some folks may seem,

There's good in all, it's true

And if you treat them as your friends

They'll be good friends to you.'

And so at last 'twas time to go,

The guests, in ones and twos,

Came up to give their warmest thanks

To their hosts the Kangaroos.

For the very best day they ever had

The animals all agree,

Was at little Joey's party, when

The Lions Came to Tea!!

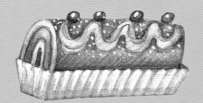

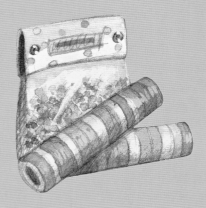